This Book Belongs To

_____

Given By

_____

Date

_____

My Very First Mother Goose Puzzle Book

Edited by Richard Mickelson

Illustrated by Patty Fleckenstein

Volume 1

Archway Publishing books may be ordered through booksellers or by contacting:

Archway Publishing
1663 Liberty Drive
Bloomington, IN 47403
www.archwaypublishing.com
1 (888) 242-5904

Because of the dynamic nature of the Internet, any web addresses or links contained in this book may have changed since publication and may no longer be valid. The views expressed in this work are solely those of the author and do not necessarily reflect the views of the publisher, and the publisher hereby disclaims any responsibility for them.

Any people depicted in stock imagery provided by Thinkstock are models, and such images are being used for illustrative purposes only.
Certain stock imagery © Thinkstock.

Edited by Richard Mickelson
Illustrated by Patty Fleckenstein

ISBN: 978-1-4808-4954-9 (sc)
ISBN: 978-1-4808-4955-6 (hc)
ISBN: 978-1-4808-4956-3 (e)

Printed in China.

Archway Publishing rev. date: 8/30/2017

I dedicate my part of this book

—to—

Patty Fleckenstein
for the great pleasure
she gives to those who enjoy
her remarkable drawings.

Richard Mickelson

Introduction

Puzzle: A question, problem, or contrivance
designed for testing ingenuity — Webster

Ever since time began, people have been puzzled by the stars, the oceans, the earth, and many other things. Is the earth flat or round? How far across and how deep is the ocean? What lies beyond the stars?

My Mother Goose book is filled with puzzles that allow children to use their minds and come up with solutions. It teaches them about life situations.

Mother Goose, as we know her, is more than 500 years old. She dates back to the mid-seventeenth century and came to America in 1787 — the year the United States Constitution was signed.

Today, there are more than 700 Mother Goose rhymes, stories, and riddles. She has become very much a part of America. Virtually every child in the world has been introduced to Mother Goose and can recite many of the most popular rhymes. Humpty Dumpty, Jack and Jill, Little Jack Horner, and others are heard wherever there are children playing.

Originally, there were only twelve nursery rhymes. Authors worldwide have added to this list. Two of the rhymes in this book, Three Little Pigs and Little Red Riding Hood, are originals written by me.

I've had fun researching Mother Goose during the past several years and have not found anything like *My Very First Mother Goose Puzzle Book*. This book contains forty-eight rhymes and twenty-four incredible illustrations.

The fun and puzzles begin when you read the rhymes and enjoy the pictures. Each picture contains a unique visual blending of two nursery rhymes. It's up to the reader, no matter what age, to decide which characters in the pictures go with each rhyme. The last few pages in the book contain more fascinating puzzles and provide directions on how to solve them, assuming you can! If the children are too young to solve the puzzles in the back, they can enjoy the first part of the book and try to solve these puzzles when they are old enough. I have shared the puzzles with older children and adults, and I cannot describe the fun they had trying to solve them. Try them on your family and friends.

My Very First Mother Goose Puzzle Book, Volume 2 is in the making and will be ready for publication at a later date. Enjoy this amazing journey. It will bring you love, laughs, and fun!

Table of Contents

List of Nursery Rhymes

Alphabetical List of First Lines

Baa, baa, black sheep have you any wool?

Brother pig number 1 built a house of straw, number 2 a house of sticks.

Do you know the muffin man, the muffin man, the muffin man?

Georgie Porgie pudding and pie . . . .

Goosey, goosey, gander, where do you wander?

Here we go round the mulberry bush . . . .

Hey diddle, diddle! The cat and the fiddle . . . .

Hickety, Pickety, my black hen . . . .

Hickory Dickory Dock . . . .

Hot cross buns! Hot cross buns!

How much wood would a woodchuck chuck . . . .

Humpty Dumpty sat on a wall.

I'm a little teapot short and stout . . . .

Jack and Jill went up the hill to fetch a pail of water.

Jack be nimble.

Jack Sprat could eat no fat.

Little Bo-Peep has lost her sheep . . . .

Little boy blue, come, blow your horn.

Little Jack Horner sat in the corner.

Little Miss Muffet sat on a tuffet . . . .

Little Red Riding Hood went to her grandmother's house to bring her wine and food.

Little Tommy Tucker sings for his supper.

London Bridge is falling down . . . .

Mary had a little lamb. Its fleece was white as snow.

Mary, Mary, quite contrary . . . .

Do you know the muffin man, the muffin man, the muffin man?

Old King Cole was a merry old soul . . . .

Old Mother Hubbard went to the cupboard . . . .

One, two, buckle my shoe.

Pat-a-cake, pat-a-cake, baker's man . . . .

Pease porridge hot, pease porridge cold. . . .

Peter, Peter, pumpkin-eater . . . .

Peter Piper picked a peck of pickled peppers.

Ride a cock-horse to Banbury Cross . . . .

Ring a ring o'rosies.

Round and round the cobbler's bench . . . .

Rub-a-dub-dub, three men in a tub . . . .

See-saw, Margery Daw . . . .

Sing a song of sixpence, a pocket full of rye . . . .

Sister Sue sells pretty seashells down by the shore.

Star light, star bright . . . .

The itsy bitsy spider went up the water spout.

The Queen of Hearts, she made some tarts . . . .

The Sandman's coming in his train of cars . . . .

There was an old woman who lived in a shoe.

This little piggy went to market.

Three blind mice! Three blind mice! See how they run!

To market, to market, to buy a fat pig . . . .

Twinkle, twinkle, little star . . . .

Nursery Rhymes
and Pictures

Hickety Pickety & Humpty Dumpty

Hickety, pickety, my black hen,
She lays eggs for gentlemen.
Gentlemen come every day
To see what my black hen doth lay.

Humpty Dumpty sat on a wall.
Humpty Dumpty had a great fall.
All the king's horses, and all the king's men
Couldn't put Humpty together again.

How many eggs can you find in the picture?
How many bells are on Humpty Dumpty's hat?
How many butterflies do you see?
How many yellow stars can you find?
What color are the chicken's feet?

Hot Cross Buns & The Muffin Man

Hot cross buns! Hot cross buns!
One a penny, two a penny, hot cross buns!
Hot cross buns! Hot cross buns!
If you have no daughters, give them to your sons.

Do you know the muffin man, the muffin man, the muffin man?
Do you know the muffin man, who lives on Drury Lane?
Oh, yes, I know the muffin man, the muffin man, the muffin man.
Yes, I know the muffin man, who lives on Drury Lane.

How many cats do you see, and what colors are they?
How many gingerbread figures are on the shelf?
How many people do you see wearing blue shirts?
What colors are on the tablecloth, and what color is the boy's hat?
How many muffins is the man touching with his fingers?

The Queen of Hearts & Pop Goes the Weasel

The Queen of Hearts, she made some tarts,
All on a summer's day.
The Knave of Hearts, he stole the tarts,
And took them clean away.

Round and round the cobbler's bench,
The monkey chased the weasel.
The monkey thought it was all in fun,
Pop goes the weasel.

How many hearts are on the queen's dress?
How many bells are missing from the queen's crown?
How many animals can you find?
How many roses do you see?
How many boots have bells on them?

Pat-A-Cake & Little Jack Horner

Pat-a-cake, pat-a-cake, baker's man,
Bake me a cake as fast as you can.
Pat it, and prick it, and mark it with B,
And bake it in the oven for baby and me.

Little Jack Horner sat in the corner,
Eating his Christmas pie.
He put in his thumb and pulled out a plum,
And said, "What a good boy am I!"

How many green legs do the table and chair have?
How many plums are on the boy's thumb?
How many pies and cakes are in the picture?
What color is the girl's ribbon, and where is it?
Who is wearing glasses and a baker's hat?

Pease Porridge Hot & I'm a Little Teapot

Pease porridge hot, pease porridge cold,
Pease porridge in the pot, nine days old.
Some like it hot; some like it cold.
Some like it in the pot, nine days old.

I'm a little teapot, short and stout.
Here is my handle. Here is my spout.
When I get all steamed up, hear me shout.
Just tip me over and pour me out.

How many teacups can you find?
How many blue pots do you see?
How many cats are in the picture?
What colors are on the teapot?
Where are the fork and three spoons?

Three Little Pigs & Little Red Riding Hood

Brother pig number 1 built a house of straw, number 2 a house of sticks.
Big brother pig was a lot smarter and built a house of bricks.
The Big Bad Wolf, to eat the pigs, blew away the houses of straw and sticks.
Pigs 1 and 2 ran to the house of bricks, as it could not be blown away.
Wolf went down the chimney into a boiling pot, vowing, "I won't stay!"

Little Red Riding Hood went to her grandmother's house to bring her wine and food.
When the Big Bad Wolf threatened to eat Grandma, she said, "How can you be so rude?"
A huntsman passing by heard what they were saying and shot the Big Bad Wolf dead.
Then Little Red Riding Hood and Grandma happily drank the wine and ate the bread.

How many pigs can you find?
What is Little Red Riding Hood carrying?
Where is the straw house with a blue door?
Where is the wolf, and what color is it?
How many animals are in the picture?

Hickory Dickory Dock & Three Blind Mice

Hickory Dickory Dock,
The mouse ran up the clock.
The clock struck one. The mouse ran down,
Hickory Dickory Dock.

Three blind mice! Three blind mice! See how they run!
They all ran after the farmer's wife,
Who cut off their tails with a carving knife.
Did you ever see such a thing in your life as three blind mice?

How many mice are chasing the farmer's wife?
How many mice are wearing sunglasses?
How many mice are running up the clock?
How many mice are not wearing jackets?
How many hearts are on the top of the clock?

One, Two, Buckle My Shoe & Itsy Bitsy Spider

One, two, buckle my shoe.
Three, four, knock on the door.
Five, six, pick up sticks.
Seven, eight, lay them straight.
Nine, ten, a big fat hen.

The itsy bitsy spider went up the water spout.
Down came the rain and washed the spider out.
Out came the sun and dried up all the rain,
And the itsy bitsy spider went up the spout again.

How many shoes are on the boy's feet?
How many pink pillows do you see?
How many flower pots with purple flowers can you find?
What color is the spider, and how many legs does it have?
What color is the downspout?

Peter, Peter, Pumpkin-Eater & Jack Be Nimble

Peter, Peter, pumpkin-eater,
Had a wife and couldn't keep her.
He put her in a pumpkin shell,
And there he kept her very well.

Jack be nimble.
Jack be quick.
Jack jumped over
The candlestick.

How many orange pumpkins can you find?
How many candlesticks are there, and who is jumping over one?
Where is the green pumpkin, and who is hiding under it?
What color are the boy's star and the candlelight?
How many pumpkin stems are there and which one is the biggest?

This Little Piggy & To Market

This little piggy went to market.
This little piggy stayed at home.
This little piggy had roast beef.
This little piggy had none.
This little piggy said, "Wee, wee, wee!"
All the way home.

To market, to market, to buy a fat pig,
Home again, home again, jiggety jig.
To market, to market, to buy a fat hog,
Home again, home again, jiggety jog.

How many pink pigs can you find that are wearing a dress?
How many gray pigs are there, and how many pigs are wearing jackets?
How many pigs with hats on their heads do you see?
How many pigs have buttons on their coats?
How many pigs are eating ham dinner?

Little Boy Blue & Baa, Baa, Black Sheep

Little boy blue, come, blow your horn!
The sheep's in the meadow; the cow's in the corn.
Where is the little boy who looks after the sheep?
He's under the haystack. He's fast asleep!

Baa, baa, black sheep have you any wool?
Yes sir, yes ma'am, three bags full,
One for my master and one for my dame,
One for the little boy who lives down the lane.

How many bags of wool are there, and what color are they?
How many sheep are black with a red ribbon?
How many fence posts can you count?
What color is the bale of hay, and what color is the boy's hair?
What is in the little boy's lap, and what can you do with it?

Mary Had a Little Lamb & Little Bo-Peep

Mary had a little lamb. Its fleece was white as snow,
And everywhere that Mary went the lamb was sure to go.
It followed her to school one day, which was against the rule.
It made the children laugh and play to see a lamb at school.

Little Bo-Peep has lost her sheep,
And can't tell where to find them.
Leave them alone, and they'll come home,
Bringing their tails behind them.

How many sheep do you see in the picture?
How many sheep are wearing flowers?
How many sheep are hidden in the corn?
Where are the big pink heart and the school bell?
How many books is Mary carrying, and what colors are they?

Old King Cole & Rub-A-Dub-Dub

Old King Cole was a merry old soul,
And a merry old soul was he.
He called for his pipe, and he called for his bowl,
And he called for his fiddlers three.

Rub-a-dub-dub, three men in a tub.
And who do you think they be?
The butcher, the baker, the candlestick-maker!
And all of them going to sea!

How many people aren't wearing hats?
How many people are wearing hats?
What are the three fiddlers wearing?
How many men are in the tub, and who are they?
What is the king sitting on, and where is his beard?

See-Saw, Margery Daw & Little Miss Muffet

See-saw, Margery Daw,
Johnny shall have a new master.
Johnny shall earn but a penny a day,
Because he can't work any faster.

Little Miss Muffet sat on a tuffet,
Eating some curds and whey.
Along came a spider, who sat down beside her
And frightened Miss Muffet away.

Where are the bowl and spoon?
Where is the see-saw, and how many children are playing on it?
What color is the girl's hat, and what color are her shoes?
What color is the spider, and what is it doing?
How many yellow pieces of clothing can you find?

Ride a Cock-Horse to Banbury Cross & Here We Go Round the Mulberry Bush

Ride a cock-horse to Banbury Cross,
To see a fine lady upon a white horse.
Rings on her fingers, and bells on her toes,
She shall have music wherever she goes.

Here we go round the mulberry bush,
The mulberry bush, the mulberry bush.
Here we go round the mulberry bush,
On a cold and frosty morning.

How many mulberry bushes are there?
How many children can you count?
Where is the white horse, and who is on it?
What color is the hobby horse's head?
Where is the castle, and what color is it?

Ring a Ring O'Rosies & Georgie Porgie

Ring a ring o' rosies,
A pocket full of posies.
Ashes! Ashes!
We all fall down.

Georgie Porgie, pudding and pie,
Kissed the girls and made them cry.
When the boys came out to play,
Georgie Porgie ran away.

How many children are wearing purple clothing?
How many children are wearing yellow clothing?
How many children are wearing hats, and what colors are the hats?
How many kids are wearing green suspenders?
What color stripes are on Georgie Porgie's pants?

Little Tommy Tucker &
There Was an Old Woman Who Lived in a Shoe

Little Tommy Tucker sings for his supper.
What shall we give him? White bread and butter.
How shall he cut it without a knife?
How will he be married without a wife?

There was an old woman who lived in a shoe.
She had so many children, she didn't know what to do.
She gave them some broth without any bread,
Then whipped them all soundly and put them to bed.

Where is the old woman, and what's she standing on?
Where is the loaf of bread, and what's next to it?
How many children are climbing the shoestring?
How many children are wearing something red?
How many children are looking out of a shoe eyelet?

Peter Piper & Woodchuck

Peter Piper picked a peck of pickled peppers.
A peck of pickled peppers, Peter Piper picked.
If Peter Piper picked a peck of pickled peppers,
Where's the peck of pickled peppers that Peter Piper picked?

How much wood would a woodchuck chuck,
If a woodchuck could chuck wood?
If a woodchuck could chuck wood,
He would chuck as much as he could.

How many butterflies do you see?
What colors are the hat and the pants?
How many sticks is woodchuck holding with a leaves on them?
What color are the leaves on the tree, and how many leaves are on it?
What is Peter Piper picking in the garden?

Mother Goose Says, "Let the Puzzles Begin."

Hello, my lovable friends. This is Mother Goose asking you if you have heard or read my nursery rhymes. If you have, then it's time to find out if you can solve my puzzles. Here's how you do it.

There are forty-eight nursery rhymes and twenty-four pictures. As you know, every picture contains two nursery rhymes. I have put together a silly two-line rhyming statement for each of the pictures. You must pick two rhyming statements located within the boxes and find the picture that matches them. Here's how it works. Picture one includes the black hen, Hickety Pickety, and Humpty Dumpty. Can you determine which two rhyming statements best describe this picture? If you can't do it, here's the answer:

She sometimes lays ten eggs at a time and really doesn't know how.
Answer: Hickety Pickety

From high on the wall came a screaming egg and hit the street, KAPOW!
Answer: Humpty Dumpty

Now it's your turn. Remember that the rhyming statements and pictures are in a scrambled order, so you have to search for the answers. Every two rhyming statements are in a box, and that box will solve the puzzles. Good luck!

HONK, HONK, HONK,
Mother Goose

Puzzle Challenge

She sometimes lays 10 eggs at a time and really doesn't know how.

From high on the wall came a screaming egg and hit the street, KAPOW!

A peck of pickled peppers was devoured each evening before bed.

He chucked the wood into the fire and said, "I'm way ahead."

Her fingers and toes make music, no matter where she goes.

As they ran by the mulberry bush, the air was cold upon each nose.

His pipe lay on the table; for his bowl he would merrily call.

A butcher, a baker, a candlestick maker, a tub will hold them all.

Snow white sands made her drowsy as she hummed a happy tune.

And looking out her window, she saw a cow jump over the moon.

There are ovines in the meadow and bovines in the corn.

Three more bags of black wool, and the sweater can be worn.

The little girl going off to class, her lamb she wants to show.

Their tails were left behind them as homeward they did go.

Posies in our pockets, we circle the bushes, and all fall down.

Kissing girls makes them cry. The boys chased him out of town.

There are little piggies all around. Five may be living in your shoe.

Pigs in the market, nice and fat, will make a wonderful stew.

Two teetering on a board is a very funny game to play.

A girl and a spider saw each other, and she quickly ran a-whey.

She stared in wonder at the little star twinkling high up in the sky.

And she wished for another happy day, as she gave a contented sigh.

A little lad waited impatiently and began singing for his warm supper.

She scolded the children soundly, "To your bunks, lower and upper."

The man who lives next door keeps his wife in a pumpkin shell.

He jumped so low the candle burned his pants. My, what an awful smell!

Lunch was over. The clock struck one; the mouse ran out the door.

The farmer's wife ran after them. Their tails aren't there anymore.

Here comes cold water tumbling from a pail carried by two.

Their diet was of lean or fat; nothing else could they chew.

My trousers are drawing blackbirds. Is it my pocket full of rye?

The cupboard did not yield a bone, and the doggie said goodbye.

Patty me a cake and make it sweet. I will not leave a crumb.

Who's that little boy in the corner with his thumb inside a plum?

One was wandering upstairs, downstairs, all around the house.

Another was gathering seashells and selling them with her spouse.

The queen made strawberry tarts, but not a one could be found.

We heard a rice and weasel pop. It was quite an unusual sound.

Three came huffing and puffing from homes of straw and wood.

Another was in Grandma's nightgown, and one wearing a riding hood.

One, two, the buckle on my shoe somehow has come undone.

A spider washed out of the downspout and made a hasty run.

Hot buns with frosted crosses were on the table for all to share.

Who made those wonderful muffins with taste beyond compare?

My fair lady ran away from the bridge as it was tumbling down.

As it landed in the flowery garden, it made quite a contrary sound.

Cold porridge in the pot, nine days old, looks very yucky to me.

I whistle a happy song, while brewing spicy, sweetened tea.

Mother Goose Nursery Rhymes Answer Key

If you can't figure them out, turn this page upside down to find the answers:

Nursery Rhymes	Page
Pease Porridge Hot & I'm a Little Teapot	18
London Bridge & Mary, Mary	30
Hot Cross Buns & The Muffin Man	12
One, Two, Buckle My Shoe & Itsy Bitsy Spider	32
Three Little Pigs & Little Red Riding Hood	24
The Queen of Hearts & Pop Goes the Weasel	14
Goosey, Goosey, Gander & Sister Sue Sells Seashells	28
Pat-A-Cake & Little Jack Horner	16
Sing a Song of Sixpence & Old Mother Hubbard	22
Jack and Jill & Jack Sprat	20
Hickory Dickory Dock & Three Blind Mice	26
Peter, Peter, Pumpkin-Eater & Jack Be Nimble	34
Peter Piper & Woodchuck	52
Sandman & The Cat and the Fiddle	56
See-Saw, Margery Daw & Little Miss Muffet	44
This Little Piggy & To Market	36
Little Tommy Tucker & There Was an Old Woman Who Lived in a Shoe	50
Mary Had a Little Lamb & Little Bo-Peep	40
Little Boy Blue & Baa, Baa, Black Sheep	38
Ring a Ring O'Rosies & Georgie Porgie	48
Old King Cole & Rub-A-Dub-Dub	42
Ride a Cock-Horse to Banbury Cross & Here We Go Round the Mulberry Bush	46
Twinkle, Twinkle & Star Light	54
Hickety Pickety & Humpty Dumpty	10